Buried Treasure

Contents

Island Life 2

Yuri's Find 10

Yuri Goes for Help 18

Yuri Learns a Lesson 22

Written by Ned Osakawa
Illustrated by Xiangyi Mo and Jingwen Wang

Island Life

Yuri had lived on a small island all her life. When you live on a small island, there aren't a lot of things that you can do for fun. But that didn't stop Yuri and her friends. They always found things to do. They had fun and they were never bored.

One of the things that Yuri liked best of all was going to one of the island's many beaches. When she wasn't doing schoolwork or helping her parents, she would go to the beach.

Yuri loved the sand. It was soft and as white as sugar.
She built castles in the sand, all shapes and sizes.

Yuri and her friends took turns burying each other in the warm sand.

They often walked barefoot along the wide sandy beaches, hunting for unusual shells.

When one of the girls found a large shell, she would hold it to her ear and listen for the sound of the roaring ocean.

One day Yuri went to the beach by herself. While she was digging in the sand, she struck something hard. At first she thought she had hit a big rock. She kept digging around it. Soon Yuri could see that it wasn't a rock. She still couldn't see what it was, but it was definitely large.

"I wonder what it is," she said to herself, very excited.

Yuri got down into the hole and began brushing away more sand.

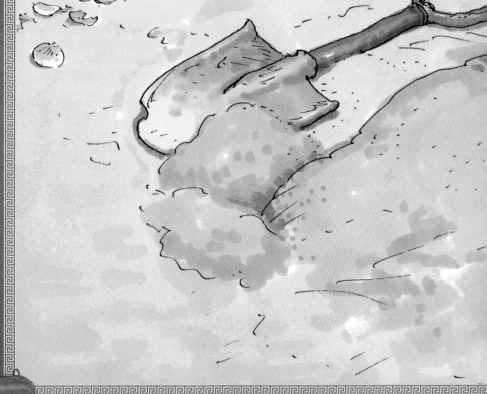

Before long, Yuri could see that the object was made of wood and metal. She wondered whether it was part of a shipwreck that had washed up onto the beach during a storm and had become buried in the sand. Or maybe it was a treasure chest buried by pirates!

Yuri's Find

Yuri's excitement grew as she dug. She clearly could see that it wasn't part of a shipwreck now. She kept digging. She could almost see the shape of the object. It began to look more and more like a treasure chest. Her heart was beating fast.

"It is a treasure chest!" she yelled.

Yuri tried to pull the large chest out of the sand. She tugged and pulled with all her strength, but the chest was too heavy and was buried too deep. She dug away more sand and again tried to pull the chest out of the sand, but it would not budge.

11

Soon, Yuri was worn out from trying to pull the chest out of the sand, so she gave up and went for help. She found six of her friends and returned to the beach with them.

When her friends saw the treasure chest, they got excited, too. They couldn't lift the chest out, so they got some ropes and tied them to the chest. They also got two thick poles and used them to help pry the chest from the sand. They tugged and pulled and moaned and groaned.

It took them almost an hour to get the chest clear of the sand. A rusty lock held the lid tightly closed.

"Now what?" asked Yoko, as they lay exhausted on the sand. "We can get to the lock, but how are we going to open it?"

"I'll get that big rock over there," said Yuri. "The lock is old and rusty. It shouldn't take too much pounding to break it open."

"Hurry! Hurry!" they all shouted. "We can't wait to see what's inside!"

Yuri's best friend, Hiromi, was the most excited.

"I'll bet it is full of sparkling diamonds, shiny gold, and glistening silver!" she said. "Yuri, you'll be rich, and you'll be able to buy whatever you want!"

"Don't get your silly hopes up," said Yuri. "It's probably full of rocks and old rusty nails."

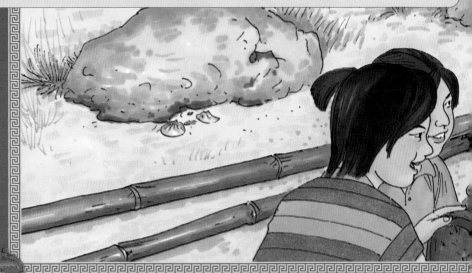

Yuri began pounding on the lock with the large rock. It was awkward banging on the lock while she was crouched down in the hole in the sand. When she got tired, Hiromi took over. It wasn't long until the lock popped open.

Yuri's friends crowded around in anticipation, their eyes wide open as Yuri slowly lifted the lid. Hiromi was right! The chest was filled with gold, silver, and diamonds. Yuri couldn't contain her excitement.

She jumped up and down, yelling, "I'm rich! I'm rich!"

17

Yuri Goes for Help

Yuri asked Hiromi, Yoko, and her other friends to guard the treasure while she ran home to tell her parents the good news.

She ran into the house, shouting, "You won't believe what I've found!"

"With all the excitement I hear in your voice, it must be something very good," said her mother, sipping her tea.

"You bet it is!" said Yuri. "Better than anything you could ever imagine."

Yuri's father looked at her with doubt in his eyes.

"I suppose you're going to tell us you dug up some hidden treasure," he said with a smile.

"That's exactly it!" said Yuri. "How did you guess?"

"I was just kidding," replied her father in surprise.

"Well, it's no joke," said Yuri. "It's for real, and now we're the richest family on the island!"

Yuri's parents looked at her very strangely.

"We are very happy for you," said Yuri's mother, "but you will have to excuse us for a minute."

Yuri's parents stepped outside the house and began whispering. Yuri could not imagine what they were talking about.

"What do we tell her?" whispered Yuri's mother. "She doesn't know the rules of the village. She will be so disappointed when we tell her that she can't keep the treasure for herself."

"She's a smart girl," said Yuri's father. "She'll understand when we explain."

They went back into the house to talk to Yuri.

"Yuri, we live in a wonderful village," Yuri's father began to explain. "I'm afraid your treasure belongs to everyone in the village, not just to us. It's our tradition to share whatever is part of the island with everyone on the island."

Yuri stared at her parents. "I found the treasure. It's only right that it should belong to me!" Yuri said, and she ran out to the front porch, tears welling up in her eyes.

Yuri Learns a Lesson

Yuri's father followed her. He sat down beside her and began to explain.

"Yuri, I know this is difficult to understand," he said. "You've been to the docks, and you've seen how the fishermen share their catch with everyone?"

Yuri nodded miserably.

"You've seen how those who are able to pick coconuts from the tall palms share them with those who can't climb so high?" her father asked gently. "Those who have fruit trees always share with us, because we have none."

Yuri looked at her father and nodded thoughtfully.

Her father went on. "The freshwater stream is on another man's land, but it is there for everyone, isn't it?"

Yuri smiled, and nodded.

"The world is for sharing," her father said gravely. "We all share the warmth of the sun and the light of the moon."

Yuri began to see the importance of sharing and began to feel better about sharing the riches she had found. She squeezed her father's hand happily.

"Come on," she said, "I'll show you the treasure."

So Yuri led the way to the treasure chest. Her parents, with help from all the children, loaded the heavy chest onto a cart and pulled it back to the village.

When they reached the village, Yuri and her friends helped her parents place all the gold and silver coins, along with the diamonds and other gems, onto a large mat woven out of grass. The village elders began to count the coins and the gems. They knew that the village was now very rich.

Everyone in the village celebrated. They sang songs of thankfulness and danced happily through the narrow village streets. They cheered for Yuri and showered her with beautiful flowers.

The next day the village elders met to discuss what to do with all the wealth they now had. They voted to build a new school. And a new library. They would also build a new hospital.

There were many good things that they could do with the money. Life on the island would be better than ever.

To thank Yuri, the villagers carried her through the village in a special chair. She felt like a queen.

When she passed through the village, people placed fruit and flowers in baskets that hung from the chair. Yuri felt very special. She had learned that sharing the wealth of the treasure was far better than keeping it for herself.

Despite all the attention she got, Yuri remained the same girl she always was. She still liked playing on the beach with her friends, Yoko and Hiromi. Every day they would go to the beach and dig in the sand. But as hard as they searched, they never found another treasure chest.